The Amish Baker's Suitor

Sadie Weaver

D1715229

Contents

Chapter 1

♥

Hard work never killed anybody, her mammi used to say.

Usually, Katie would agree with the statement but with her arms smarting under the weight of the basket and her vision wavering from the heat, she would not be faulted for choosing to dismiss the authenticity of such advice in this critical moment.

The day started out well enough. Katie arose with the crows at dawn, quickly making her bed and pegging some clothes on the line before rushing inside to *redd up*. Soon, she started her twenty-minute morning walk from the house to the bakery, the hem of her gown flapping between her legs and the breeze lapping at the straps of her gray apron as she hurried along the gravel-beaten path.

Katie's Bakery was situated in the center of town, at the end of a long row of shops. The shops catered to both the local Amish population and visitors who occasionally wandered into Willow Valley. Across the street, directly in front of her bakery was a craft store owned by one of Katie's very good *freinds*.

It was Beth who helped her procure some of the dairy products from Jacob's farmhouse and Beth who was also manning the buggy to fetch the products from the farmhouse. The horse – an old stable mare –proved difficult and Beth had a hard time keeping it out of the potholes.

If Katie hadn't been in a similar predicament, she would have laughed at Beth's poor attempt to control the animal.

As it was, she was trying to extricate the corner of her apron which was snagged on the door handle, wincing at the pain that shot up her arm when the wood brushed against the burn on her hand.

"Jahveh!" Katie exclaimed when the door suddenly sprung open in her face. The items in her straw basket

fell out as the basket was jerked out of her hands. The fruit rolled out on the steps, bouncing down the walkway and into the street. "*Nee*." She darted after the fruit, ramming her head into the wall closest to her. A breath whooshed out of her.

Today was not her day.

"You've hurt yourself," a deep, unfamiliar voice called out.

"*Och*, we should go after those items," Katie muttered, her attention still on the fruit rolling away.

"In a bit," the voice was cool and calm. The door closed behind her and soon, she found herself led to one of the chairs under the awning outside her bakery.

"The *gut* Lord knows we should not let those items go to waste when we can preserve them." Katie wasn't ready to let it go. She parted ways with some good ol' barter bucks in exchange for those fruits. The heel of her palm rubbed the side of her head where she hit it.

As if disagreeing with her words, a buggy passed, and the hooves of the horse squashed many of the fruits into the gravel. Katie sighed and fell back into the chair, shoulders slumped.

"Katie," Mary, one of the town's oldest residents smiled down at Katie from where she sat in the box seat. "Will you be coming to the barn raising on the morrow?" Next to her, Harold – one of her grandchildren – held the reins impatiently.

"I might. *Och*, I don't know. I have some chores..." her voice trailed off when Mary's gaze bounced off her and jumped to the man beside her. She gave the duo a look of intolerance and rode on. Katie didn't know what to make of that.

"Glad to see Mary hasn't changed." A chuckle followed the departure of the hoofbeats.

Katie turned to the stranger with a questioning look in her eye. Her cheeks were red and glistening with sweat from the heat of the gas oven, and her *kapp* was lopsided, some tendrils of her hair slipping out. "Mary is an *alde* sweetheart," Katie said fondly. She was about to ask if he knew the *alde* woman but when Katie looked at him, she promptly forgot her question.

He had a long, lean face. His eyes were the color of the clear pond located at the back of her barn. He had a strong jaw that hinted at a strong will – a bit of stubbornness too – and a wide mouth.

Her gaze returned to his eyes once more. Those eyes – there was a depth in them that revealed an abundance of experiences as if he had seen the ugly side of life one too many times.

Her gaze traveled down to his hand resting casually against the top of the rickety chair. Calloused hands: the hands of a man who wasn't a stranger to manual work.

Mammi would approve.

The thought jumped into her head at the same time she realized she was staring at the man.

Gut Lord.

"You are not from around here, are ye?" Katie rubbed her palms down the skirt of her gown, averting her gaze and trying to hide her unabashed scrutiny of the poor man.

"I could answer both ways. My name is Levi." He looked at her as if she should immediately recognize him.

He did look familiar though.. something about the nose and chin? And those eyes... But Katie attributed it to seeing so many walk through the bakery. Faces blurred together, sometimes.

"Levi?" Katie gave him a small smile, fiddling with her *kapp* and getting it back into place. Her gaze moved to the approaching buggy and she saw the form of her friend, Beth. She made a move to rise but saw Levi curiously watching her and remained seated. She liked looking at him, she realized. His features were very appealing.

He had broad shoulders and judging from her encounter with the door and her head, she knew he was strong too.

"My name is Katie. Katie Fisher," she introduced herself, feeling a bit nervous for some reason.

"I know."

"You do?" A small frown pulled her eyebrows together. Before she could question how he came to know her name, the buggy pulled up next to her bakery and Beth dismounted. Behind her, another neighbor descended. At first, Katie could not see who it was.

"Katie, have you seen the bakery assistant I sent your way?" Beth was asking.

"*Nee,*" Katie answered, going around to the back of the buggy to unload some of the dairy products.

"Jane, you should not be troubled in your condition." She quickly took the milk container that the other woman was wrestling with.

"It's no trouble." Jane, a young lady of twenty-three, with long red hair and sharp brown eyes looked at Katie with a warm smile.

She also happened to be very thick around the middle, expecting a baby in a few months. She was wearing a green dress and matching apron, with a white *kapp* neatly tucked on her head.

"My husband is still in the barn. He will be along very soon. I also dropped a message with the Lander boys, they are busy with the barn raising for tomorrow, but they mentioned some of their friends will be along in some minutes." She was panting by the time she was done.

"I think you should get out of the sun and off your feet." Beth, the oldest of the three women, came forward to help the pregnant woman to the rows of chairs, one of which Katie just vacated.

"*Denki* you ever so much," Jane was saying. "Everybody knows how kind and generous you are, Katie, so you should not bother about having your hands full."

"*Jah. Denki* you for the kind words. The pastries are still in the oven. Once they turn golden, I will put in the next batch," Katie said, walking alongside Jane.

Early in the month, towards the end of winter, Jane informed her that she would be holding a community event and she wanted Katie to provide catering services.

Katie saw Levi standing off to the side, his black felt hat in his hands and immediately felt guilty for ignoring her visitor.

"I am sorry, Levi. Jane here is having guests over for a community gathering tomorrow and it's an all-hands-on-deck situation. We wouldn't mind if you volunteered."

Levi's face scrunched up with an indecipherable expression. He shuffled from one foot to the next.

The reason for his bizarre attitude became clear the next instant when Jane spoke.

"*Bruder*, what are you – what are you doing here? I thought you were at the barn."

Bruder? Katie looked from one to the other. It suddenly made sense to her, that odd familiarity when she looked at him.

He was Jane's brother. So that made him not just any Levi, but the notorious Levi Yoder... the one who left and didn't return.

Next to Katie, Beth stiffened, a hard look entering her eyes. The woman's lips thinned but she didn't say anything.

Everybody in Willow Valley was old-fashioned, but some were more old-fashioned than others. Beth included.

Levi looked at Katie first before turning to address his sister. "Well, you were busy loitering in the kitchen, and I thought to help you get ready."

Jane nodded and said, a bit sharp, "Thank you, *bruder*, but we've been managing just fine." *Without you*. Jane did not say that part out loud, but they all heard it. It was right there on the tip of her tongue, and in her eyes.

Katie quickly glanced at Levi, saw his closed-off expression, and decided it was her responsibility to step in and lighten the mood. By all looks, Levi had just returned from his very extended *Rumspringa*, and she was well aware of the cold treatment to which he would be subjected. There was no helping it.

"As I informed Levi, we need all hands on deck. No use turning help away." She glanced at Levi. His expression was still shut down, but she thought she detected an iota of relief.

"Missus Katie…" Two rough figures appeared some feet away, squinting and elbowing each other. They were gangly teenagers – Lander's boys. The Landers owned the guesthouse in town and were always willing to lend their boys out to whichever neighbor found themselves in need of help.

"Oh. Right on time." Beth motioned them to the back of the buggy. "Be careful with the crates of eggs. They cost a leg and an arm." The boys grunted out a response as they got to work.

The door to the bakery swung open and the fryer stepped out, his face red and sweaty. There was grease all over his apron and some on his face. He was huge, standing at least a few inches taller than Levi, whom Katie thought was the perfect height.

"The scones are all done. The donuts are in the proofing cabinets. You may have a look at the scones to see if they are nicely made."

Katie took a whiff of the air. The July air was mild and pleasant. The smell of bread and baked goodies drifted in the air, tantalizing the neighbors and luring them in. "Half of the batches are to go to the town's elders, right?" she glanced at Jane to confirm if that was still the case. "While the other half will be shared amongst the youngsters in the schoolhouse?"

Jane nodded. "Rightly so. Let me just confess that I am mightily craving one of those pies of yours."

Katie chuckled. "As you should."

Beth stepped forward, latching gently onto Jane's hand. "We will help ourselves to some if you don't mind."

Katie smiled convivially. "Not at all." She glanced at the Lander boys and gestured them over, "Go on, you may have your fill of some of the pies too."

With the two women and boys out of earshot, Katie turned to Levi. He was holding her basket in his hand now and was filling it with whatever fruit he could salvage. Better something than nothing.

"Here. You might need to rinse them."

Katie accepted the basket gratefully.

"And maybe you ought to take care of that burn." He gestured towards her bruised hand.

"What – oh. *Jah. Denki.*" Katie smiled, a blush rising to her cheeks. It wasn't until she was giggling that she realized she was a bit nervous standing next to this man. "Do you care for some pie? Donut?"

Levi shook his head, staring intently at something on Katie's forehead. "Don't go to the trouble."

"It's no trouble." Even as she said it, the forgotten ache in her arm returned but she hid it away. "You've just returned from your... *trip.*" She cleared her throat. "It's only fair that we treat you to some care and pampering."

"That would be a first," he informed her. Levi tried to make it a light banter, but she heard something deeper in his tone. Not wishing to probe the source of that entangled feeling, she smiled brightly at him, feeling the intensity of his gaze roam her face.

"I wouldn't be too quick to judge. If you let people, they just might shock you," she said, ducking her head and glancing at him from under her lashes.

Chapter 2

♥

The fair was exactly as he remembered; resplendent, crowded, and rowdy. There was nothing to compare it to. It filled him with an uneasy nostalgia.

The air was alive with the smell of freshly baked pies and the sound of fiddle music playing in the background. Colorful booths selling everything from hand-crafted goods to apple ciders to delicious foods lined every side of the street. People of all ages were milling about, enjoying the beautiful weather and the simple pleasures of life.

At the end of Levi's booth was Sam – Levi's one-time best friend. They attended *singeons* together for years. Now Sam was married to the bishop's *dochder* who was expecting their first child.

Across from Levi was Jane. Her hair was packed tight-ly in her *kapp* and she had a huge smile on her face. She was laughing with her son and handing roast corn to the boy and his friends. The sun shone brightly, capturing the joy on their faces in one bright moment. Levi felt the sense of community and togetherness, almost palpable in the air, and he quickly looked away.

Moving to where the reed and grass materials hung from the ceiling of the booth, he selected an unfinished basket and got to work coiling the strips of grass around the core center.

"*Onkel?*"

Levi heard a young voice followed by some giggles and shuffling. He looked behind and saw boys barely older than four years of age outside his booth, flashing their milk teeth. He recognized one of them as his nephew – Josiah – the boy had his mother's dark complexion and his father's mop of blond hair. The *kinner* had been dragging Levi's shoe bag around the *haus* earlier, earning a rebuke from his mother.

"Josiah." Levi sat down. "Who are your friends?"

"Michael and Eli."

Levi glanced up a minute before spreading the fabric and bark on his covered thighs. "That is *oll recht.* Bring me the awl...and the flint knife. Careful."

The boys rushed to do his bidding. "What are you doing, *onkel*?" Eli, the tallest of the boys asked curiously. His mother was Jane's friend growing up and Levi saw the resemblance on the boy's face. Leah had been a pretty girl and he almost courted her once. She didn't quite intrigue him – too set in her ways, he used to think.

Unlike the other...

At the intrusion of the thought, he shied away from it. There was no place for any of the regret that plagued him in Florida.

"I am making a coiled basket."

"I never seen it made this way," one of the children observed, taking a step closer while Michael, the other boy hung back.

"That is because I do not use lye. I use water. It helps to preserve the natural fiber." He looked at the boys and saw their attention on the other items in the booth, but he carried on. It was somewhat pleasant having ears to talk to. Non-judgmental ears.

"Isn't it wonderful?" Josiah called out proudly, looking at his other friend. He bit into the roast corn, sending chaffs of the snack to the ground.

"I don't know." Michael, with a sulky face, looked down, using one foot to make circles in the sand. "My *mamm* told me to be wary of strangers."

Josiah frowned in that adorable way that children were prone to. "My *onkel* is not a stranger, isn't that right, Eli?"

Eli looked at the older man before responding timidly. "*Jah*. He is no stranger. He was born here," the boy stated as a matter of fact.

"But then he ran away," Michael insisted, not looking up yet.

Ah. So that is what they've been telling these young ones. "I am back now, and I am going nowhere. You can tell your mother that."

A loud ruckus came from one of the other booths where a lot of children were gathered around Katie Fisher for snickerdoodles and shoofly pies. She had a large jar in her hand and was busy handing treats to one child after the other. Next to her, her friend Beth and an unfamiliar man were helping with the other snacks. The man was wearing a muted gray button-up shirt and slacks, he also had a well-worn hat on his head and seemed at ease in the setting. By all indications, he was a Mennonite.

Levi looked around him. No eager customers or passersby were stopping to haggle prices or drop some neighborly compliments. He sent the children off and made his way to the other woman. Levi admitted that he could not resist going to her even if he tried.

"At this rate, I am afraid there will be nothing left to serve the guests at the party." Levi stopped directly in front of Katie's booth, looking down at the cluster of children and young teenagers who immediately shuffled around on their feet.

"We will make do," Beth grumbled, a hard look on her face. Next to her, the Mennonite glanced at the other stranger with curiosity.

Katie paused a moment. Beads of sweat formed on her forehead and wisps of her hair plastered around her face. The weather started out cool enough but was fast turning warm under the watchful rays of sunlight. However, the look of delight on Katie's face at Levi's presence could not be mistaken. "Levi, I was just asking your *schwester* about your whereabouts. *Wie ghets?*"

"*Gut*. Very *gut*. Was minding my business over there when I saw you and decided to come to offer my help. If it's needed." He pulled on one strap of his suspenders to adjust it.

"*Jah*. It is needed. It is *gut* of you to offer. We're getting *redd up* to head to your *schwester*." Katie glanced around her. "Have you met Eben? He's Beth's beau from Indiana. She invited him over for the frolic at your place."

"Pleasure to meet you." The two men shook hands. Levi observed the relaxed look on the other man's face and eased up a little. The children reared up, ramming into the men before they raced off in the direction of a toy booth in the distance.

"Children...*och*! You haven't any choice but to love them, isn't that right?" Katie stared after the children who disappeared in between booths and the moving crowd. She dusted her hands on her apron. Emotion thickened her voice for a second, but she cleared her throat, and her expression cleared. "Beth and Eben will be riding a-ways in a few minutes. I was hoping you'd be available to help transport some of these containers and leftovers to the bakery." Then her eyes flitted to his booth and her shoulders drooped, "I completely understand if you have your hands full with your booth, though. Jane told me you were hoping to make some sales with the baskets."

An irrepressible itch started at the base of his neck, and he scratched it. "Er...it...well...I'm not entirely sure I will be missed for the rest of the day."

While the other lady snorted and averted her gaze, Katie, with her flushed face and soft amber eyes gave him a look full of understanding. "*Ach*, you should have seen me sometime last summer. It was not pleasant. The first few weeks of opening a business are usually the hardest, I have discovered. But believe me, it'll change."

She sounded too convinced that he couldn't bring himself to explain that her situation was very different from his.

Beth interrupted with a loud voice to be heard above the din in the background. "If you'd like me to stay, Katie, you've only to say the word."

Katie smiled warmly, flashing strong white pearls. "Sure, I do. But you've been very helpful these past few days. I can't possibly ask you for more. Besides –" she looked at Levi, eyeing his sturdy appearance. "I think I'm in *gut* hands."

Beth didn't share Katie's faith in the stranger but the *Gelassenheit* – the practice of acceptance amongst the Amish – mandated that they welcome one and all, provided doing so did not jeopardize their beliefs. "If you say so."

Levi nodded stiffly. "Excuse me. I'll go close up shop and grab some of my things."

Soon, the two adults were shuffling containers and hurling thermal coolers into the back of the buggy. It wasn't until the sun was setting that they finally started their journey back to Kate's bakery.

On their way out of the fair, the elderly woman by the name of Missus Mary gave them both apple ciders, while darting intense scowls his way.

The evening sun was setting slowly, casting a warm glow over the surrounding fields and farms. The sky was streaked with brilliant pink, orange, and purple and the shadows were lengthening. The air was still and peaceful, interrupted only by the hooves of the horses along the road and crickets in the bush.

"I've missed this," Levi was saying, his eyes closed and his head thrown back against the seat.

"Willow Valley or the people?"

"A little of both," he responded immediately and she knew the answer came from deep within him.

She wiggled a little in her seat. "It is a wonder to me then that you stayed away as long as you did." At her statement, his head shot up to hers. "*Jah*. I might have...might have probed a little. It doesn't hurt to do a little neighborly research," she completed without taking her gaze off the horses.

"Research?" he spewed the word as though it was foul. "And what have you found out?"

She slid him a queer look. "Nothing beyond what I already assumed."

"And what's that?"

"That you still have people loyal to you even though you might not believe it."

Now he was the one averting his gaze. He reined in the horses when they neared a ditch, and then the silence continued. Just when she thought he wasn't going to respond, his voice filled the space between them. "I wouldn't blame anybody if they all hated me now."

"I don't think they do. They might be smarting over your prolonged absence but that's only to be expected."

Levi nodded but didn't say a word until they were parking outside her house. "*Kumm* on, I'll help you down."

"*Denki*," Katie held onto the bodice of her gown as she alighted. There was a moment between them as they stood eye to chest, and then she broke away.

The path leading from the street to the front of the steps was beaten down and illuminated by the stars that were beginning to dot the sky.

"Once you are done unhitching, would you mind coming in for a cup of water? Or *kaffe*? Then we'll be on our way to your *haus*."

"Water," he said after a long pause. "Water would be *wunderbar. Denki.*"

Chapter 3

♥

For the next few hours, Levi found himself mired in running errands.

By the time he and Katie arrived at his family home, the house was in full swing, voices raised in chorus. Beautiful voices blended in with the sounds of clapping in every corner of the house, and gas lamps cast light from tabletops in corridors and hallways.

While they might treat him like an outsider on a normal day, there was no excusing him from joining in the Singing and the Grace that followed where scriptures were read out loud and discussed.

Quickly, Katie and his sister put him to work sharing pastries while more were being baked in the kitchen.

"I thought he might have returned by now," one of the visitors was whispering to the other visitor next to her.

"Heard him tell his *schwester* that he wasn't leaving anytime soon. I think something happened with his Englisher beau, the one he left us for years ago."

One part of the Amish culture that Levi wasn't particularly fond of was the small-knit gossip that he was often subjected to. His sister might have dropped a few details about his personal life and that fodder was circulating throughout the town.

His eyes caught something to the side and he saw Katie observing him from a doorway. Like magnets, they gravitated toward each other.

"You're all done?" he enquired and she shook her head.

"Still have several batches to go but there's one batch in the oven now."

The smell of baking *brode* and pies along with woodsmoke drifted through his nostrils, reminding him that he hadn't taken anything of substance since the day broke.

He nodded and slid next to her, looking out into the living room where the laughter of people reverberated in the room.

"I'm sorry, I couldn't help but overhear some of ..." her voice trailed off.

Once again, he nodded, still looking straight ahead. She was bound to hear sooner or later, he was glad it was now. Like most Amish women, she might not be outspoken but she would not hold back in giving her opinion, he knew and awaited her harsh criticism.

"For what it is worth, I am sorry about what you went through."

An apology was the last thing he expected to hear. Slowly, he turned to watch her, scrutinizing her face for any signs of her true feelings. Though her features were not clearly visible under the dim lighting, he was still able to make out that lovely face full of impossible kindness. "Why?"

"Why?" She looked straight into his eyes, understanding all he was asking even though he wasn't able to express himself in so many words. "Because I know a thing or two about loss, and that you should never be blamed for going after your heart's desires."

If those words had come from the lips of an *Englischer*, he would have considered them open-minded. Hearing those words from a fellow Amish made him believe there was such a thing as miracles. "Katie, you... there is nothing quite like it. I loved her, I'm not ashamed to say." His voice dropped. "What I am ashamed of is allowing my love for her to nearly cost me my *familye* and my community – that precious bond."

Now she turned slightly so she was facing him, her hands crossed across her bosom. "Maybe it's time to look forward instead of living in the past and regretting decisions that have already been taken."

Levi stepped closer to her. It was only natural that he took her hand in his, mesmerized by the difference between them. His hands were strong and callused while hers were just as strong, but delicate and exquisite.

"Levi..." she started, her voice getting quite husky.

"I would like to court you, Katie Fisher, but I'm afraid there might be someone to whom you are already pledged." Matter of fact, he was concerned that was a very real possibility. Men would be swarming around her and he wondered why she wasn't yet married. She was beautiful, strong, kind-hearted, and so devoted to her work and faith. Beyond that, there was something special about her that he couldn't put a finger on.

Wordlessly, she shook her head, equally mesmerized by him.

Out of nowhere, two people appeared next to them. One was his sister and she looked quite happy about their coziness. The other person, not so much.

"Katie, everyone is talking about how *appenditlich* your pastries are. They are asking for extras. We have also sent some of the batches to some folks that could not make it here tonight."

Katie nodded. There was a strained look in her eye that wasn't there seconds ago. "*Denki*. We are running on the last of our supplies. I already sent for more, which should have arrived half an hour ago. Frankly, it has me a little worried but I'm sure it's nothing to be concerned about."

"Are you sure? I could send Dan to check up on your supplier and see what's going on."

"I'm sure it's nothing to worry your husband about."

"It would be no bother. We're all involved."

"Perhaps I could go in your stead to see what is going on," Levi volunteered.

"I know the country much better, let me go. I'll take my fastest horse and will be back before you know I'm gone," the other man interjected. There was a hard, unflinching look in his eye that had Levi wary.

Katie looked from one man to the other and simply remarked. "It is most generous of you to both offer but I'm sure there's no need."

Jane saw the two men watching each other and quickly made the introduction. "Levi, meet Jacob Stoltzfus, he owns one of the largest dairy farms in Willow Valley. Jacob, meet my *bruder*. Have to check in on Josiah. I can't leave that boy for one second." She left them with a promise to be back.

Growing up, Levi did not socialize much, so there were many of the town members he didn't know. He extended his hand to shake that of the other man. The handshake was not a friendly one between the two of them.

"Katie, you've been working hard all day. I looked for you at the fair but by then, you had left already. I hope you aren't tiring yourself out?"

"*Denki* ever so much for your concern. I've had help from everybody, even Levi here."

Jacob brushed off that last part of the sentence as though it hadn't been spoken. "*Vell*, you know everybody in Willow Valley has always been there for you. We don't need any outsider to show up for you."

That was a jibe and it was as obvious as the evening stars apparent through the open windows. Katie felt it was up to her to clear the air. "Since there are no outsiders in here, I'm sure you are right. I have been doing fine with everyone's help." There was an emphasis on 'everyone.'

Jacob moved from one foot to the next. Jacob was one of Willow Valley's respected residents. He ran a dairy business, supplying milk, cheese, and yogurt to the townspeople.

Physically, Jacob was slightly taller than Katie, with large eyes that were one of his best features. His hair was muddy brown and he was beginning to grow thick in the middle. He also had that softness about him that belied the hardworking front he tried to present.

Everybody knew the Stoltzfus clan were not rich from hard labor but rich from business acumen and doggedness. Though, business savvy was it's own sort of hard work and it was commendable, really, what they'd built.

What Katie didn't find commendable was his attitude lately.

"I'm sure," Jacob muttered. "If you aren't too busy afterward, I've been meaning to drop by sometime this week to discuss some business with you. After all, we have to prepare for Harvest which is almost upon us."

"Please, feel free to drop by anytime. I'd be happy to have you," Katie replied good-naturedly and Jacob swelled with joy. "Now if you'll excuse me, I have to go back to the kitchen. Hope to see you around later on."

Jacob didn't look ready to let her go but she was out of his sight before he could say anything about it. He scowled at Levi before returning to the living room.

Levi thought it funny though, the way the man tried to bully him.

Katie peeped from the kitchen doorway mere minutes later. "Levi, is that offer still available? One of the neighbor's children just informed me that the supply cart is caught in a ditch and will not be able to make the last leg of the trip down here."

Levi frowned. "How far away is it?"

"Just outside of town." She looked worried. "My assistants called in sick a couple of hours ago and now this." She looked well and truly fed up. "And I don't want to involve any of the visitors in any of this." Her hands were covered in flour.

Levi nodded. "Do you know what? Give me the exact location. I'll get my buggy and quickly make the trip."

"But, Levi, you might be making more than one trip. I am so sorry about this."

He hovered a hand at her shoulder for a fleeting moment. "Please, let me do this for you. I find it refreshing to contribute in any way I can. I'll take Dan with me as well, I'm sure he won't mind."

She touched his arm lightly. "*Denki* ever so much, Levi. You've been very helpful. I'll keep a plate for you before it gets all eaten up."

"That would be nice, considering I haven't had anything to eat all day."

She looked surprised. "*Och*, why didn't you say anything? Wait. I'll be right back." She returned with a big plate of creamy mashed potatoes, roast chicken, some veggies, homemade jam, and fresh bread. "Please have this before you go. I'll get you a cup of fresh tap water. And maybe some fry pies to munch on your way." She fretted over him in that typical way that his mother used to.

"*Jah. Denki.*" He accepted the hefty plate, resisting the urge to lick his lips. It looked absolutely delicious.

Chapter 4

♥

It wasn't until Katie was changing her dress for the third time that she finally admitted to herself that she was nervous and might be overdoing things a little.

She spent more than twenty minutes brushing her hair until it glistened and shimmered with the sheen she desired. Next, she scrutinized the sleeves of her gown and the skirt, to be sure her dress was spotless.

It was some days after the community gathering at Levi's house and she hadn't seen him since. She recalled that night and how helpful he had been. It was several hours later before he finished the trip. She truly admired a man who got things done.

She invited him to a quilting bee that she was participating in and beamed with joy when he accepted.

"I'd like to court you," his words that night came back to her and she squirmed, remembering the heated look in his eye when he informed her of his decision. For the rest of the night, they didn't speak of that matter again as they were both too busy attending to everyone. She realized that she never did have the time to give him an answer. He might think she already pledged her love to somebody else if she left it at that.

There was a time when everybody was certain that she and Jacob Stoltzfus were going to be together, and actively pushed the idea. While she laughed it off, Jacob had not found it in the least humorous and made it plain that he wanted to take their casual friendship a step further.

At that point, she made it clear to him that she didn't feel the same way. Recalling his possessive attitude that night at Levi's, Katie wasn't so sure he got the message.

"So, you and my *bruder*, eh?" Jane had walked into Katie's bakery early the next day, with a glint in her eye and a spring in her steps. "I never quite pictured it but now that I think about it, you two would make the perfect couple, you know?"

Katie had blushed heavily at the time and quickly moved behind the cabinet to gather her utensils. Thinking to keep her hands and mind busy, she was quite unprepared for the images that popped up in her head from Beth's colorful words.

How would it feel to be a couple? Her and Levi – together? *Walking through the neighborhood holding hands, exchanging looks, laughing at insider jokes.*

Now, Katie walked briskly down the dirt-beaten path, she sighted the buggies parked outside the Gales' sand-house and held tighter to the basket containing her sewing supplies and some pies – cherry, chocolate chip cookies, and bread for the get-together. Theo, her assistant would be bringing over the vegetables, dumplings, scalloped potatoes, and bread pudding that he made at her behest.

They were having a quilting bee to celebrate the new babe in the Gales family. For the longest time, Mary and Finnegan had been without children, and the good bishop had to minister to them on more than one occasion to keep the faith going.

Everybody in Willow Valley was happy to hear that Mary put to bed a set of healthy, bouncing baby boys.

As she approached the *haus*, she heard laughter and murmurs from inside. Her cheeks pushed up with her smile.

"Knock, knock." She looked through the door net, seeing a hazy view of the living room. There were four women seated near the hearth, heads bowed in concentration as they gushed over fabric in the center.

One of the women looked up and smiled when she saw Katie. "Oh, *gut*. You are here. *Kumm, kumm.*" She rose to her feet and ushered Katie inside. "You may place that here, *denki.*" She assisted Katie in placing the basket on a table just below the window.

Katie rubbed her hands up and down on her apron. "Hope I'm not too late?" She took off her leather shoes and placed them neatly next to the door.

"*Nee.* We were just about to start. You're right on time." Sylvia grinned at the younger lady. Sylvia happened to be Mary's sister-in-law, a former resident of Willow Valley before she moved out of town with her husband.

The other three ladies waved at Katie and bid her welcome.

"Did you bring some needles? I left mine on the table back home."

"*Jah*, Priscilla. I came with some needles." Katie went to rummage through the basket and returned a minute later.

"*Kumm*. We need your advice." From beside Priscilla, Deborah Brooke gestured to Katie, a look of concentration on her fair face. Deborah was married to the *bischop* and the black austere gown she wore underneath the white apron gave away her position. Deborah was also beloved by everybody in town and her daughter was expecting her first child in some months.

"I'd be happy to give it." Grinning, the bakery owner rushed forward.

"So, we have a bit of difficulty deciding the pattern to go with. We need a tie breaker. Priscilla wants us to do nine-patch while I am more inclined to do stars. We've agreed to do a bit of piecing and then some quilting but the matter is, we are yet to decide the design. Stars or nine-patch?"

Katie looked from Deborah to Priscilla, about to ask why Sylvia wasn't voting.

"Oh, *nee*. My opinion carries no weight. I'm not a Willow Valley resident. Or so I've been told," Sylvia answered the question that was clear in Katie's eyes. Sylvia lived just outside of Willow Valley, where Katie grew up. Katie was always visiting her *mammi* in Willow Valley and only moved in fully to take care of her during her later years.

Katie bit the inside of her lip, trying to see if Sylvia was upset. Only curiosity and light humor were reflected in those eyes looking back at her. Katie clapped her hands and pretended to be immersed in her very important decision. "Uhm, I'm going to have to go with Deborah on this one. The last one we did during Thompson's burial was Nine-Patch. Sorry, Prissy."

Priscilla waved her curly hair to the side, "Oh, sure. Was just having a grand time being the difficult person for a change. Mary already hinted she wanted stars."

Katie looked around the small living room and saw the curtains blowing in the breeze. The room contained only practical furniture. Some sofa chairs, a table, a leg stool, and some pillows strewn here and there. Once again, the hot afternoon breeze thrummed through the interior. Katie's cloth stuck to her back as trickles of sweat ran down her bodice.

Using a hand to stir up air, "Can I check in on the new mother?"

"Sure. By all means. She'd love the extra pair of hands."

"All right."

As always, Katie was awed by the miracle of babies. They were a delight to her. She loved the way they looked, the way they smelt, and the way they felt when you held them in your hands. She spent the next two hours with Mary. For a moment, the thought of carrying her own child drifted through her mind. A child that had suddenly acquired gray eyes and black hair in her daydream. Katie blanched when she realized she was picturing her child in the image of a certain gentleman across town.

By the time she returned to the living room, more women had arrived. Women from all over town flitted in and out of the room, carrying baskets with colorful quilts that provided a blend of brightness in the area. The windows had been opened completely to let in the pitiful breeze blowing through the house.

Katie was about to join some of the women working on the quilt padding in the corner when she caught sight of the bishop – Deborah's *mann*.

Quickly, she made her way to him, pausing when he exchanged pleasantries with a few of the other women.

"*Bischop* John?"

Bischop turned and squinted to observe Katie. The bishop was in his late forties, his hairline was beginning to recede but his gaze remained as sharp as ever. He was in his black frock coat, and black stock fastened at the neck, he wasn't wearing his black apron or black hatband, probably as a result of the weather.

"Katie. I was just asking the *gut* sister about you."

"I've been inside, helping Mary."

Bischop John pulled Katie towards the less crowded end of the room. "It is most kind of you to help your brethren when they require it but who is helping you? Last I heard, you've been very busy with projects all over town." He folded his hands behind him and the pages of *die Botschaft* – the weekly newspaper serving the Old Order Amish – rustled behind him.

At his attention, Katie blushed. "You don't have to worry about me, *Bischop*. I get by quite *vell*."

"I am happy to hear that. I know you had the most difficult time adjusting after the death of your *mammi*. I would hate for you to feel neglected in any way." He searched her eyes for any telltale signs.

Under his kind gaze, she squirmed, unable to avoid some of those feelings from slipping past her barriers into the broad daylight but she was adept enough to mask the look before it alarmed the good *bischop*. "I have to say, those first few months weren't the easiest but with time…" she lifted her shoulders. "Everyone has been very helpful, *du* as well."

He nodded, pleased. "You will be around for the *Die Gebet* on Sunday? I would love to share some scriptures with you. I noticed you came in late on two occasions."

She chortled, half embarrassed and half-amused to have been caught by the man of *Gott*. "I will take care to *kumm* in earlier, *Bischop*."

He gave her a fond look, "*Da Herr sei mit du – Gott* be with you, Katie."

Katie went on to exchange small talk with the other women, occasionally laughing at their harmless gossip.

Chapter 5

For the third time, Levi reconsidered his decision to drop by unannounced during a community gathering.

Katie invited him, though, and it would be extremely rude to turn her down without a reasonable explanation. As of now, his only explanation was that he felt uncomfortable and at odds in this setting. But he was an adult, and he could not leave a lady hanging.

As he stood rooted in front of the open doorway, he looked from one female to the next, shuffling restlessly on his feet.

Finally, Katie walked by and noticed him. The smile that beamed brightly on her face was worth all the angst he endured.

"Katie."

"Levi, you're here. What – what are you doing standing out there?"

"I was just about to..."

She didn't let him finish as she pulled him inside. "I was beginning to think you weren't coming anymore."

He cocked his head to the side and smiled down at the charming lady. "I already gave my word and despite how it might seem, I always try to keep it."

"I believe you." Katie gave him a playful elbow jab. "Besides, what's in that knapsack you are holding?" She asked with mild curiosity.

Levi glanced down at his hand. "*Och, jah*. It's a keepsake. I made it for the *bopplin*."

Katie's mild curiosity deepened into a stronger one. She clapped her hands excitedly. "Can I see it? I know I'm not supposed to do that but please, can I? It will be a small peek."

Levi laughed at her preschool excitement. "*Oll retch*. See for yourself. Two rocking horses. I carved them myself." He lifted his hands to the light and she saw the light blisters on the inside of his palm at the same time, she saw the wooden caricatures. The attention to detail in his work of art was second to none. He was speaking before she could compliment his talent. "Perhaps you'll be kind enough to give it to Mary on my behalf?"

Katie snorted. "Oh, *nee*, you are not wiggling out of this. You will give it to her yourself."

Before he could protest, they were already strolling towards the new mother's room at the end of the hallway. As they walked past, some snickers could be heard.

Furtively, Katie looked at Levi to see how he was reacting to the snickers. If he was concerned, it didn't show on his face. "Mary and Finnegan will love it, I know."

He nodded. It was only when he turned away slightly that she observed the dark circles under his eyes. At the entrance to Mary's room at the end of the hallway, she paused with a hand poised over the door handle. "Did you stay up all night making that?" A low whisper emanated from her.

He nodded. "I wanted it to be perfect. Mary taught me in eighth grade and she was always very welcoming."

Though he tried to brush it off, she saw right through him then and there. He acted like a gruff bear with a devil-may-care attitude but she could see it was mostly a front. "Still, doing this...it's a kind gesture."

He started to say something but then the door opened from the inside and the glowing face of Mary appeared. "Katie...Levi..."

"Hallo. Sorry to bother you but Levi here dropped by to wish you well. He also has something for your boys."

As it turned out, the parents were delighted by the gifts. Mary had tears in her eyes as she accepted them, applauding the wonderful craftsmanship. Some of the women thawed in their cold treatment of Levi and warmed up to him in no time.

It might be slow but to Katie, that was progress.

By late afternoon, Katie was ready to call it a day. She had a small crick in her neck from bending over the table for hours. All in all, she was overjoyed to have Levi next to her.

Levi was completely enthralled by the event. From the leather padding to the quilting to the designs, the quilting bee was a harmony of community solidarity.

Soon, Levi convinced Katie to let him walk her home. After saying their goodbyes and ignoring some of the fixed looks and pointed remarks from the others, she admitted that she enjoyed having him around.

For some reason, they meandered through town and somehow ended up in Willow Creek, where the crickets cricked amidst the ribbiting of the frogs. Here, the atmosphere was cool, and not even the heat of the day was overly present.

They sat on the bank of the river where the sides were blanketed by pine trees. A gentle breeze teased the water, causing soft ripples on the surface.

Katie sat down, head thrown back and eyes closed. The pressure she had been under for the past few days slowly drifted off of her. "I could stay out here all day long," she remarked.

Levi watched her, amazed by her beauty. As the direction of the breeze changed, it brought with it the scent of her perfume and all he wanted to do was scoot closer to better take it in. "Before I left for my Rumspringa, this was my favorite spot. Over there, my *dat* taught me how to fish and I took great delight in it."

The emotion in his voice caused Katie to open her eyes and watch him. "You miss your *dat*?"

He slowly nodded. "Jane informed me you recently lost your *mammi*."

At the mention of her *mammi*, Katie's expression sobered, and she looked away. "She was ill for the longest time. I'm glad she's at rest now."

"I didn't mean to bring up painful memories." Levi hesitated, but carried on, "It's just...I would like to know more about you. I did ask to court you, Katie, but so far I haven't heard a response. Why do you suppose that is?" His voice was soft, gentle, and unobtrusive. "I understand if you don't have an answer for me yet."

Twin splotches of red settled on her cheeks, giving her a rosy cherub appearance. "Er, it's... er.."

A masculine hand settled on top of hers. When she looked at Levi, the look in his gray eyes seemed to calm her nerves. "Like I said, Katie, please, you don't have to give me an answer right away."

Somehow, tendrils of courage she didn't know she possessed kicked up to the surface so that she felt confident enough to squeeze his hand on hers. "I already have your answer."

If she hadn't been so keen on watching him, she would not have caught the look of apprehension that flitted through him. Obviously, her response meant a great deal to him so she took care to phrase her words properly. "I have a *bruder*. He's been out of town for some time, working on a job somewhere in Indiana." She paused, then carried on. "Very often, he'd drop in but he rarely stays for long. When you were shunned, I... I understood what you were going through because I went through something similar with my *bruder*." She paused again, delighted by the air on her skin, caressing her face and pulling playfully on her hair. "When he made his decision to keep his outside job, he was met with great rebuke. Not quite as severe as yours but still..."

He nodded, listening attentively to her words, giving her room to put her thoughts together. Without conscious effort, he lifted her hand, amazed by the petite fingers. Strong and exquisite, he mused. He took it as a good sign when she didn't pull her hand away. "What of your *mamm*? Jane told me she went to visit your *bruder*."

He appeared to be close to his sister if she was bringing him up to speed on town affairs. Katie also appreciated the effort he took to find out more about her. She had done the same thing. Quietly, of course. She didn't want to stir up any unnecessary rumors until she was sure where she stood with him. "*Jah*. She'll be back very soon. Usually, she stays in the other wood house by the Cornell's field. I moved away from there sometime last year to look after my *grossmammi* before she passed on." Katie suddenly smiled. "Ya know, you would have liked *Mammi* Rose, and she would have liked you too. She always used to say you could tell a *mann's* heart by his eyes. The eyes are, after all, windows to the soul."

"A wise woman." Levi smiled, appearing very handsome in his simple black shirt and trousers. "And what do my eyes tell you?"

Her hand lifted to touch the side of his face lightly and she leaned in close. "That you've been hurt one too many times but you still hold onto that goodness inside you. You are a *gut mann*, Levi. Never let anyone tell you otherwise."

The look in Levi's eyes became heated. Time seemed to stop in that moment as they both stared into each other's eyes. Kindred spirits... drifting alone in the world, both nursing some hurt and both struggling to find the light at the end of the tunnel. Perhaps, they could find it together.

"*Denki*, Katie. I appreciate your kind words."

His words penetrated the fog that weaved around her so that she quickly dropped her hand to her side, grabbing some blades of grass underneath her and tugging on them to keep her hands busy. "I only speak the truth."

"Katie..." He started but stopped. "I have to tell you something before you give me your answer. When I was outside Willow Valley on my *Rumspringa*, I... I met and fell in love with a girl. Her name's Rachel. She was a simple countryside lady, or so I thought." His features settled into a frown as he delved into the past. "We were planning on getting married but then something happened and things didn't work out. Do you understand?"

That was news to her but she nodded. "When you say something happened, what do you mean?"

"If you don't mind, I'm not up to talking about it just yet."

"She hurt you?"

"*Jah*. But that is in the past. She's moved on, I've moved on." He looked at her by his side and quickly qualified. "Or at least I'm trying to, if you give me a chance."

"I'm willing to give you a chance, Levi."

"Really? *Och*. That is very *gut* news indeed." His whole face lit up at her response. "Jane will be so pleased.

She told me you were going to accept but I'll admit I've been nervous all day."

Katie chuckled. "You and me both." There was a moment of silence before she broke it. "There will be some resistance though, I hope you know?" *And I hope you are prepared?*

"Sure. From many like your folks and others... Jacob Stoltzfus comes to mind. "

Katie was about to ask what he meant but quickly surmised. "Your *schwester* told you about Jacob?"

"Actually, my *schwester's* husband, Dan told me. Apparently, Jacob once asked your *mamm* permission to court you."

She didn't know that. How was it that she had never mentioned it? She would have to ask her when she returned. "*Mamm* never said anything. Maybe she suspected I wouldn't have agreed."

"You don't like him?"

"*Nee.* I like someone else." And then she smiled and Levi knew peace unlike any he ever experienced.

Yes, there will be troubles along the way, but he was ready to face them with her.

Chapter 6

♥

For the next couple of days, Levi and Katie looked for every excuse to be in each other's company. It wasn't easy setting up rendezvous and meetings and avoiding the shrewd gazes of the community elders and gossip mongers.

A few rumors were circulating about their newfound closeness, but Katie was less than concerned. She was fully savoring the feeling of being pursued by a man she desired.

It was on one such busy afternoon when she was attending to several customers that she caught sight of her beau amongst the crowd. He was standing under the awning, by the side. He gave her a slow smile that had her insides in knots within seconds. Thankfully, nobody noticed the exchange.

It was the beginning of September. The area boasted lush, green landscapes and the fields were filled with crops such as corn, wheat, and hay. Passing through the roadsides, you would see wildflowers scattered here and there, and the gardens were overflowing with vegetables and fruits, with leaves occasionally dropping from trees under skies that were clear and blue.

People were milling in and out of her bakery, making scheduled arrangements in preparation for the upcoming harvest. It was a beautiful time in Willow Valley.

"Katie, darling, are you okay? You look flushed." A caring hand rested lightly on her back and Katie nearly jumped.

Laughing shrilly, she glanced over her shoulder and threw what she hoped was an acceptable version of a vague smile at her pastry assistant. "Just so, Bren."

"Katie, I haven't received my order." One of the residents eyed her impatiently. "It's as hot as lava in here. I do not want to stay here any longer than I have to. Will you be a darling and speed things up a bit?" Mary, the older resident remarked, stirring up a breeze with the makeshift paper hand fan she grabbed from the top of one of the display glasses.

"You will receive your order very soon," Katie murmured monotonously, signaling to her assistant to push the woman's order to the front of the line. Everybody knew what a trouble-loving croon Mary was and how she delighted in creating explosive scenes. The weather was too hot to be saddled with cooling off tempers.

Once again, Katie glanced outside as she rushed around with a large bowl and a half-sack of flour. Levi was no longer standing by the side but bent over one of the chairs on the sidewalk.

What was he doing?

Quickly, Katie brushed oil on top of each bread dough before loading the tray into the wood-fired oven. She grabbed a dishrag and made a beeline for the exit.

Katie ducked her head against the sunlight. Overhead, the bell jingled. Levi looked up and stood to his full height.

"What are you – doing?"

"The chairs." Levi shook the top of one chair and then another. "It's just *kumm* to my attention that a lot of these chairs have gone rickety."

The woman rubbed a hand across her forehead, smudging herself with flour. "*Jah.* I've been meaning to change those chairs, but I never have the time to get around to it."

Levi nodded. "I will help."

Katie clapped her hands. "Really? I'll pay you with a free lunch."

"That settles it then. I'll drop by tomorrow.'

It was the way he said it – so sure that she would welcome his help anytime.

Soon, the two took their seats. Across the white-surface table, Levi reached for Katie's hand. "I've missed you."

"I have missed you too." Her smile was slow and sweet. Around them, the bakery continued to bustle with customers coming and going.

"So what have you been up to all day?"

He shrugged. "You know, this and that. Mostly been out on the farm. Dan was kind enough to show me the ropes."

"That is most kind of him." Her throat felt parched. "Do you want a drink? Any drink?"

"*Jah*, please."

Katie returned with two full glasses of homemade lemonade. However, by the time she returned, Jacob Stoltzfus was sitting next to her beau with a determined glint in his eye. "K... Katie."

"Jacob, I didn't know you were around." She couldn't prevent her voice from dipping.

"Of course not." Jacob beamed like a well-fed cat who had the mouse cornered.

Katie stood hovering over them for some minutes, thinking about what to do to get rid of the new addition. "Are you...did you place an order?'

Jacob shook his head. He was wearing a black felt hat and black *brogans*. His jaw was clean, indicating a recent shave. "Will be placing one in a few minutes." He looked around. "You have to admit, Katie, you've got the Midas touch. I love what you've done with the place. It becomes you."

"*Denki*," Katie said simply. She exchanged a look with Levi when the other man looked away. She was itching to be alone with Levi. She didn't wish to talk about how her bakery business was kicking off or the new paint on the walls.

Suddenly, without a preamble, Jacob started. "I ran into your brother-in-law some days back, Levi, he mentioned he was running errands on behalf of Jane and said it won't be long now before she puts to bed." Jacob's voice was conspiratorial.

"*Och, ja.* Jane knows that she needs to slow down over the next few weeks to be safe."

"I'm sure." There was a pause. "But there's talk you might not even be there for the christening."

Katie rolled her eyes in vexation. She had had enough of his petty ramblings. "Jacob, I do not know where you heard such tall tales, but Levi will be here for a long time. It is high time we learned to accept that fact and move on." Her voice was curt. If Jacob was going to spread hateful rumors, he should go elsewhere for attention.

"It hasn't been decided...yet." Levi squirmed in his seat.

"What?" Perplexed, Katie looked from one man to the other. "What hasn't been decided?"

"Me staying."

"What?" she repeated lamely, struggling to catch up with what he was saying. "I don't understand."

"Katie, I was going to tell you. Can we discuss this later, when we are alone?"

She ignored his last request and hopped onto the first statement. "You were going to tell me you were leaving?

Levi sighed. "*Nee*. I mean, it's not been decided yet." He turned a scathing glare on Jacob who seemed to be enjoying the tension in the air. "I'm going to explain it all to you."

All Katie could do was nod. Cheeks burning with embarrassment, she stared down at her fingers. "It's *oll retch*. We don't need to have that discussion. I understand." *Understand he was toying with her heart, trying to keep himself busy before he left town again.* She only wished she hadn't gone and fallen in love with him.

"Katie..."

"I think you should leave her alone," Jacob inserted. His voice and posture had suddenly turned hard. "I do not know what sort of life you led when you left town but we do not make promises we do not intend to keep to our women here."

"Jacob, I suggest you stay out of this." Violence wasn't his way but if this farmer continued to push him, he would push back.

"And I suggest you leave Katie alone. She's had enough heartbreak in her life, she really doesn't need the instability you will bring."

Instability? The word sank into Levi's heart and his rising temper ran out. Jacob might be a lout but he spoke the truth. Levi shut his eyes. Within seconds, his voice came out sounding flat, and on his face was a stoic expression he mastered over the years. "I'll leave you now, Katie. Thank you for the drink." He looked down at the enticing lemonade that he hadn't even gotten around to drinking. "Much obliged." He rose to his feet.

Leave now? Was he leaving her now? The questions screamed in her head but outwardly, her expression was calm. With a stiff nod, she watched him leave, her heart breaking with every step he took away from her.

"I'm sorry." Next to her, Jacob shifted on his seat and reached for her hand. She didn't even have enough strength to flinch. "I know you were hoping for more from him but, Katie, you have to understand that with *menner* like that, there's nothing they can offer you except heartbreak and more heartbreak. That's not what I want for you, if only you'd see it."

But Katie wasn't. All she was seeing was the untouched glass of lemonade and the very absence of a gentleman with dove-gray eyes.

She managed to smile, even though the smile wobbled. "*Denki*, Jacob. Now if you'll excuse me, I have to go make some more bread. Please, have a drink. I made them myself." She pushed one of the glasses of lemonade his way.

Without waiting for his reply, she quickly returned to the bakery.

Chapter 7

♥

For the next few weeks, Willow Valley residents prepared for harvest. Crops were getting close to maturity. Farmers were beginning to sharpen the blades on the combine and making necessary equipment repairs.

Jane delivered a beautiful, rosy-cheeked baby girl with the most adorable toothless grin towards the end of the second week in September.

Levi threw himself into the task of making his baby niece very comfortable. The news of her birth was announced in the weekly church bulletin.

That day, they opened their home to well-wishers and family members. The tired mother tried to entertain as much as possible but she soon retired into her room, leaving both her husband and brother to keep the entertainment going, as well as keep Josiah, their young child, in check.

Levi stood on the front porch of the wood house, welcoming the guests as they arrived. The weather was cool and rainy and the leaves were beginning to change color and fall from the trees.

"I was looking for you. I should have guessed you'd be out here. She still hasn't arrived?" Dan, Jane's husband stood beside him, resting on the railing, and looking out over the front yard of the house.

"Do you think she's going to...?" Levi's question trailed off into uncertainty.

Dan, with his reddish brown hair, dropped a hand on his shoulder. "Knowing Katie as well as I do, she will be here."

Levi held onto that conviction, jumping every time he saw someone make their way towards the white two-storied building he shared with his sister and her husband.

An hour past noon, Katie arrived with her friend, Beth. Levi was seated on one of the wooden benches, quietly working on a whistle for Josiah.

The two women strode up to the house. As usual, Beth wasn't giving him an easy time of it.

"It's wonderful to know you are still here," Beth remarked, directing a contradictory look at him. "You haven't left us yet."

"Beth," was all Levi said in response. His attention was entirely on the quiet lady standing next to Beth. The half-made whistle was forgotten in his hands.

Once again, Levi admired Katie's unobtrusive beauty. If she had not chosen to live in the Amish community, she would have had a fine time running men ragged out in the world. But as it was, *Gott* kept her for him.

Katie was wearing a light sable dress with a light-colored *kapp* and a frilly pair of shoofly shoes.

She was beautiful, he thought, wondering how she was able to maintain that glow on her skin considering how hard she worked.

"Katie," he drawled her name. "It's *gut* to have you here."

Katie shrugged, unsure what to say in this moment. One thing was certain; she was overjoyed to see he was still around. The thought of him leaving Willow Valley kept her up every night.

"Your *schwester*...we came to pay a visit." Her words were broken. She was nervous and it showed in the way she talked.

"She's inside."

Katie nodded and she turned to go inside.

"Wait, Katie." Levi quickly stepped in front of her. "I'd like to speak to you. In private."

"You haven't felt the urge to do that in all this time. Why now?" Beth piped in. On her face was flippant intolerance. "Katie, let's go."

"Please..." The plea jumped out of him.

Katie bit her lips in hesitation. "Beth, you go right up. I'll be a minute."

"But...are you sure?"

"*Jah*. I'll just be a minute."

When they were finally left alone, Levi turned to her.

"Beth's right. I'm sorry. I shouldn't have stayed away. It's just...after the last meeting, you...I saw how you looked at me and it hurt."

She was quiet, letting him gather his thoughts.

"When Jacob told you I was contemplating leaving town, he spoke the truth. I did speak to Dan about the possibility and he must have heard or Dan slipped up, I don't know." He paused. "I've had time to think about it. The truth is, making the decision to *kumm* back here wasn't easy. I knew what I was getting myself into." He drew in a long breath and paced a few steps before stopping in front of her. "Then I think about you, how you picked yourself up after the death of your *grossmammi*, how you threw yourself into your bakery business, how you seem to thrive. I can't help but feel a little jealous."

Katie's hand rose to her mouth. "You're jealous of me?"

"I'm jealous of how you keep pushing. I honestly do not know where you get the strength."

Katie squinted her eyes. "I get the strength from the next-door neighbor who checks in on me every time I miss a wash day. I get the strength from the kind acquaintances who send referrals my way. I get the strength every time somebody calls my name out during *Singeon* or at a community gathering. Look around you, Levi. Everything you need is around you. You are stronger than you think and closer to that dream I can see in your eyes, the dream you somehow think you do not deserve."

"You have to understand. After...Rachel left, I thought surely I didn't deserve any good things. She..." He stopped, recalling memories from the past.

"What happened? Do you feel like talking about it?"

Levi glanced over his shoulder and saw that nobody was within earshot. He took in a deep breath. "When I left Willow Valley, it was like being let out in the open for the first time in my life. I admit, I've always been restless here. Meeting Rachel was just perfect timing. She was everything I thought was missing from my life. She was outgoing, outspoken, impulsive, and very blunt. She made me question all I thought I knew and I basked in the feeling."

Katie squirmed. It was awful hearing him talk about another woman but they both needed to hear it.

"On and on we went. Rachel isn't like any of the women in Willow Valley. Soon, we were living together and I felt on top of the world." A bitter chuckle. "It wasn't too long before I received a rude awakening and the fairytale was over."

Katie forced her lips to open. "What happened?"

"I caught her with someone else. An *Englischer*. Someone I called *freind.*" Boy, was he wrong?

"I'm sorry about that. It must have been terrible."

"*Och*, it was. But I'm glad it happened. I wouldn't have been happy with her."

Katie took a step closer to him, reached for his hand, and breathed deeply when their hands touched. *This is home,* she thought to herself. "You don't have to worry about any of that anymore."

Levi smiled softly. "I spoke to Dan's father. He happens to be my mentor. Dan met my *schwester* when she tagged along on my visits to his kind father. Funny thing is, Dan's father said the exact same thing. That it's all in the past."

"That is because it is," she reiterated. "I wrote a letter to my *mamm* as well. I didn't give her all the details but I gave her enough details to understand my plight."

"And what's your plight?"

"I don't want you to leave." There. She finally admitted it.

"Katie, I'm not going anywhere. That is what I was trying to tell you. I was having doubts about settling in but I have given it a long thought. I'm not leaving Willow Valley, but I will be moving away from here. I already spoke to Dan and we are looking for a piece of land somewhere close by. I want to settle down, start a *familye*, build my home."

The gentle lady dropped her gaze. "It's a beautiful aspiration." She weaved her arm through his and rested her head on his shoulder. "Beautiful, indeed."

Chapter 8

♥

Levi made it a point to call on Katie every evening at seven o'clock. He was not joking around anymore. On two of those visits, he ran into Katie's cousins – Melinda and Mia. He thought they were very laid-back and very accommodating.

The daylight hours were getting noticeably shorter and the temperature was undeniably cold and windy. The animals were seen meandering around the area, getting ready for hibernation in a couple of months. Leaves were turning yellow and brown, and you could scarcely walk ten steps before you crunched one under your feet.

Katie was also busy cleaning up the *haus* as she received a mail one afternoon announcing her *mamm's* arrival the day after.

From replacing the wobbly legs of the rickety chairs in her shop to restocking her supplies and purchasing vegetables by the roadside, there was a lot to be done. He used the opportunity to check in with a Mennonite agent to whom Beth's beau had introduced him, and the prospects were looking very bright. He carried Katie along every step of the way and so often, she gave him *gut* advice.

Hefting one heavy box in her hands, Katie emerged from the attic, sweaty and with the dust settling on her clothes and hair, she let out an exhausted sigh. "Guess what I found in the attic?" Despite her obvious fatigue, she looked excited.

Quickly, he lifted the heavy box out of her hands and set it down on the kitchen counter, reaching over to wipe off the line of dust on her cheek. "What did you find?"

Her cheeks colored at his intimate touch but the next instant, she was rushing out her words, her embarrassment forgotten. "Look at this. Isn't it *chust perty?*" Katie reached inside the box and brought out a long quilt, unique in its bold blend of red, purple, and green patterns. The man held up the other end. Katie traced one pattern with her long, lean index finger. "See how straight these stitches run? Melinda says that the quilt was done by one person. Our great aunt, her name was Gerty. From what I hear, she was a dreamer – industrious and resourceful but a dreamer nonetheless."

"Sounds like someone we both know," Levi said, giving her a meaningful look. Before she could respond, he went on. "It is *perty* though." Levi ran his hands along the material, feeling the soft texture. He wrinkled his nose. "Judging from how long it's been sitting in the attic, it needs a *gut* washing."

Katie chuckled. "Of course. Amongst us ladies, we are still debating who gets to keep the quilt. I found the box; Melinda touched it first and Mia was the one who pulled it out from the junk sitting on top."

Levi grinned. "A tough one."

"I have a feeling I might win this round but don't say anything *chust* yet." Her voice sounded conspiratorial like a giddy housewife exchanging fresh gossip during Sunday service.

He cracked a smile and dropped his voice when he heard footsteps bumbling down the stairs, "You have my word."

"Has Katie shown you what we found sitting upstairs in the attic?" The breathless voice of Mia, a fair, red-headed lady with dots of freckles adorning the bridge of her nose smiled up at him. She reminded him a little of his younger sister.

Levi nodded. "*Jah*, she has. I don't know who sounds more excited between the two of you."

"*Och*, it's Katie. You should have seen the way she bounded down the stairs. I feared she would topple over," Melinda laughed from behind the other cousin. Amongst the three women, Levi found Melinda to be the most outspoken. Her sandy blonde hair was parted neatly in the middle and packed into a tight bun that ended at the base of her neck. Her blue eyes were like the deep corals of the beach he once visited in faraway

Florida. Her personality was just as sparkly as the depth of the ocean.

A patch of red dotted Katie's cheeks at her cousins' inelegant ramblings.

Melinda suddenly switched topics. Brightly, she pirouetted, the hem of her gown swirling around her ankles. One day, this young lady was going to turn a poor sod's head around, Levi grinned. *Just the way her cousin was turning his head.* "Michael is going to be at the quilting circle tonight, did you know that? Mia just gave me his message."

Mia nodded, grabbing one end of the quilt to assist Katie in folding it neatly. "If you give Melinda the time of day, she is going to bore you with talk of her beau. Leave her be."

Melinda ignored the other lady and turned to Levi. "You have to be there, Levi. You and Katie both."

Katie ducked her head. "Considering that I am going to be baking for the event, my presence is somewhat a given."

Melinda smiled enthusiastically. "*Gut*. Then I can introduce you both to Michael. You are going to love him, Levi. He's the sweetest young *mann* ever. We are planning a June wedding, you know?" Looping her hand through Levi's, she pulled him along. "*Kumm*. I want to show you the flowers we will be using in the potting shed."

"Mel, darling, don't be *deerich*. Levi has better things to do than while away the time chattering about your obsession with your beau," Mia admonished. In a softer voice, she went on, "He's here for your cousin, in case you haven't noticed."

"Ach," Melinda's hands flew to her chest as she realized her folly. "*Ich*...so sorry," she mumbled.

Levi smiled congenially. "It's all right. I would love to see your favorite flowers, Mel. Maybe not today but sometime soon."

The lady seemed satisfied with that response. "We will be upstairs putting everything back in its rightful place. We don't want Katie's *mamm* disappointed when she returns."

"*Denki.* I will be upstairs to join you in a bit." Katie called after them, relieved to be finally free of her cousins' non-stop chatter. "I am sorry about all of that. They can be *vell* intense, I know." She chortled.

"I am fond of your cousins, Katie. They mean well."

Katie nodded, twiddling her thumbs. "So...I wanted to ask. Will you be at the quilting circle tonight?"

Levi glanced outside the window. Twilight was here already; the sky was awash in a soft glow of muted orange and red streaks. This was the time for dreaming – when magic floated into the air and became reality. He took a step closer to the young, beautiful lady and lifted an adoring hand to her cheek. Thoughts of closing the gap, reaching down, and kissing her soft lips drifted into his mind. He wanted nothing more than to hold her close to his heart. "I will be there," he finally blurted.

Katie drew in a shuddering breath and nodded, incapable of speech.

Levi gathered his resolve and stepped away. *All in due time*, he appeased his less rational self. She would be his very soon.

A few hours later, Levi was surrounded by well-meaning Amish residents, gathered around a bonfire. The landscape was green and pastoral, with rolling hills and wide open spaces blanketing the area. In between the farms and houses, maple trees, and oaks rose from the ground, along with wildflowers scattered here and there. The landscape felt timeless and simple.

The night unfurled its velvet cloak, and stars dotted the sky while the moonlight spilled its light over them like liquid silver. Children ran around the fire, cautioned by elders. By the side, the minister told one story after another, elaborating with his hands and words.

Katie dropped next to him, whooshing out a breath. "*Mammi* Mary is in the barn making some trouble." She handed over a plate of baked sweet cherry dessert – Katie's favorite – with a dollop of vanilla.

Levi took one spoonful of the ice-cream and oohed.

"You like?"

"I love," he corrected.

"I know, right? I enjoy this flavor more than the others. It's *mammi's* recipe. After my *dat* died, my *mamm* was at a loss on what to do to get me to stop moping around the *haus,* so she would call on *grossmammi.* The dear woman would visit us with one giant icebox and encourage me to dip my finger inside for a lick of real whipped cream." In her voice was a note of sadness. She went silent for a moment, interrupted only when one of the Landers boys came over with a large tray of casserole turkey, buttery egg noodles, and mushroom soup.

"*Denki.*" Levi smiled at the boy who nodded eagerly and left with an empty tray. Levi and Katie were seated close enough to the large gathering of merry campers that they weren't excluded from the folktales being told by the minister. However, they were seated far enough away to afford them a bit of privacy. The smell of roasted marshmallows drifted through the air.

They said a silent prayer before taking a sip of the mushroom soup.

"How is Jane and the baby? Still having trouble sleeping?" Katie rested her head against the boulder behind them, munching softly on casserole turkey.

"She is getting by. I wanted you to know that I will be meeting with the Mennonite agent tomorrow. He will be bringing over the buyer's covenant." The buyer's covenant was a document outlining the responsibilities of both the buyer and seller of real estate around these parts.

"This is wonderful – *gut*. Does this mean you've finally settled on a property? And is it in town?" Her words were tripping over each other in her bumbling excitement.

Levi grinned, his dark gray eyes sparkling under the flickering bonfire. Shadows danced and moved across the ground, fascinating the children who grabbed their sticks to prod and fuss.

"*Jah*, it is in town. You will see soon enough." He took another sip of the soup.

A shadow fell across their direct path, blocking their view of the light.

The couple looked up, squinting to make out the features of the people in front of them.

"Dan? Jacob? *Gut'n owed.*" Katie greeted chirpily. Behind the men, she caught sight of Deborah; the *bischop's* wife, Ellen Landers – the guesthouse owner in Willow Valley, and Mary. They were hovering some feet away but were looking to eavesdrop. Katie was determined not to have a scene tonight.

"Katie, *wie bischt du heit?*" Dan enquired and the lady responded absent-mindedly. Presently, she was preoccupied with watching Jacob and that fast-growing scowl on his face.

"We were *chust* talking of your wife."

"She's doin' *gut*. She wanted me to ask you when you'd be available for the farm sales she told you about some weeks ago."

Katie scooted closer to Levi. Jacob's eyes followed the movement. "I will pay her a call tomorrow to discuss it."

Jacob stepped forward. "Your *mamm*? I heard she will be returning tomorrow. I have some butter, milk powder, and eggs set aside for her. To welcome her back," Jacob added the last part when Katie gave him a queer look.

"Er...I am sure she would appreciate the kind gesture, but you know, you shouldn't put yourself to trouble."

"I do not consider it any trouble." Then he let out an exasperated sigh. "What I do consider trouble is finding this *mann* hovering around you, following you around everywhere you go like a lapdog that *chust* won't stop. It's becoming bothersome and people are already starting to talk."

Dan turned abruptly to his friend. "Mind you, that is my brother-in-law you are talking about."

"Stay out of this, Dan. Your brother-in-law or not, it is my duty to protect Katie's reputation from damage and this *mann* here isn't helping matters one bit."

Katie's anger brimmed to the surface. She jumped to her feet, her hands in the pockets of her apron. "Perhaps you fail to see that it is your unsolicited interference that is the problem here, Jacob. Who I choose to hang out with is nobody's business but mine. I choose to hang out with Levi, and you do not have any say in the matter."

"Katie, he is going to break your heart. Have you forgotten he is planning on leaving?"

The lady tried her best to remind herself that the dairy farmer only had her best interests at heart, even though some of those interests were from a selfish desire. She reeled herself in, clutching her hands. "Jacob, it is really none of your business."

"But..." he started.

"Jacob, the young woman doesn't want you meddling in her affairs." Ellen, one of the *nochbers* was closer now than Katie remembered. "She and Levi here are a couple, haven't you noticed?"

"They are not a couple," Jacob protested churlishly. If looks could kill, Ellen and her cohort would be six feet under right about now. A smidgen of hurt snuck into Jacob's eyes at the perceived betrayal. They were supposed to be on his side.

"What do you know? Levi already sent a mail to Katie's *mamm* asking for permission to formally court her. Why do you think she is coming back?" Dan blurted.

"Dan," Levi cautioned instantly, and the other man pulled up short, looking like he wanted to bite off his tongue.

What? Katie pulled to a stop. With eyes darting between Dan and Levi, she was *ferhoodled*. "Is this...is this true?"

"Katie, wait. I was going to tell you," he started, trying to gauge her expression. "Don't be upset."

"*Nee*. I am not upset. Far from it." She was still reeling from the news. Her *mamm* had not said anything in her letter about granting audience to a certain gentleman. Katie glanced around, seeing the curious faces of the *bischop*, the towns' elders, and some others. "While I am not entirely pleased with the subterfuge, I can't in all honesty claim to be displeased." Her tone of voice was smooth and unruffled.

If her rambling confused anybody, it was fine because she was just as confused.

But all was well because Levi had made up his mind to pursue her. *Praise be!*

Chapter 9

♥

The fall season was in full swing. The days were sunny and clear, and the nights cool and refreshing. The leaves on the trees were in varying shades of yellow, orange, and red, and the fields were filled with ripe, golden corn. The flowers were still in bloom, and the meadows were covered with a carpet of wildflowers.

It was the first Saturday in October – a day of fun and celebration for the whole Amish community. The day started with a parade through the village, led by *Bischop* John and featured floats – the ribbons on the wagons were particularly brilliant; the tractors were also artfully decorated, and the usual disgruntled farm animals prattled by amicably as if sensing the festive mood.

Later, there would be a gathering in the town square for a community-large meal with pie-eating contests,

rides, and baking competitions to stir up the festive spirits.

Levi arrived early to the town square, ready to make
plans for the day. He admitted to himself that he was a
little bit agitated. Katie's *mamm* arrived a fortnight ago
and he paid her a visit. Though she was courteous in
her interactions with him, he couldn't help but notice a
decidedly cold and detached appraisal behind her deep
brown eyes, much like her daughter's but *colder.*

His mind pulled him into the murky depths of the
past. Lately, thoughts of his former beau had been in-
vading his mind, largely due to the deep reflection he
subjected his mind to. He recalled penning a letter to
her, and how much trouble it had been finding the right
words to portray his feelings.

He read somewhere that confronting the past and
demystifying it could prove cathartic, so he persevered
and churned out the words. The jury was still out on
whether he felt better or worse in light of his decision.

*...I do not regret the time we spent together, and I hope
you will not begrudge me the time I am devoting to pursu-*

ing the lady after my own heart, pursuing the future that never seemed possible with you.

The last leg of his letter ran through his mind. He grimaced. Perhaps his words had been unnecessarily sentimental, he bemused.

Truly, he was focused on building a future with Katie. Already, he purchased a vast acreage of fertile farmland from the Parkers close to Willow Creek. By the morrow, work would commence on the land.

"I am so happy to hear this," Katie had jubilated when he informed her two weeks ago. "Have you informed the *bishop* about the imminent barn raising? You won't be inviting a few people but every person out there." She laughed at his funny expression. "If I have anything to do with it, your barn raising will be packed full of everybody in Willow Valley."

"Of course, you will have everything to do with it." There was emphasis on '*everything*'. She had to know that he was planning their future, and she had every say.

At his words, she sobered up. "Then I say we start getting ready with the preparation. It would have to be after the Harvest as every household is *vell* busy during this season." It was more than the words; it was the admission that she was a part of it. Her acceptance humbled him, and he knew, beyond any specter of doubt that he was making the right call by choosing her as his life partner.

So he nodded, happy to go with whatever she recommended.

Several households were indeed busy. His sister was helping their *nochbers* with husking their corn and preparing it for canning while the children were put to work pulling ears from cornstalks. The men were tasked with sharpening blades, operating the cider press, and working the machines to separate the grain from the straw.

Levi's task was stacking the crops in piles and loading them in separate bins onto wagons for transportation to the community mill. Some of the crops were ground into flour and animal feed while the rest were processed and preserved.

It was while running one of such errands that Levi was dealt a shock. He had just finished loading the wagon and was getting ready to swing into the buggy when a soft, feminine voice drifted to his ears.

The voice sounded out of place but more than that, it was familiar. He looked around, earnestly seeking the owner of the voice. It couldn't be who he thought, could it? She was a thousand miles away from Willow Valley, Pennsylvania. What would she be doing here?'

But when he looked hard enough, he saw a vision of what he thought was impossible. On the other side of the dirt road was a lady in a cashmere top and an expensive pair of denim trousers. She had a ridiculous brown hat sitting prettily on her head, and strips of hair blew out behind her like a model on a runway. She had always possessed that elegant air about her, so her poise didn't take him by surprise.

What took him by surprise was her presence here in rural, backwater Willow Valley! During their last conversation, she had spoken those words, so he was under no illusion of what she thought of his background.

Glancing around, he quickly crossed to the other side where the lady was asking directions from Leah who was here to collect her son, unfortunately.

"Thank you, Leah. I will take it from here," he stated grimly.

Leah was confused. "You know this lady? She was just asking directions…"

"Thank you. We are… acquainted," Levi returned coolly.

Leah shuffled from one foot to the other, switching her gaze between the two adults. There was something here, she thought. She ran a hand through her black curls and dabbed on a phony smile. "If you say so. Have a good day." With that, she left them alone.

Jacob forced his eyes not to follow the lady, knowing she would be relaying the news of the stranger's visit to the first person who asked her as soon as she collected her son and was out of there.

Rachel looked at him from under the brim of her hat. He saw traces of smudged eyeshadow. "So, acquaintances, huh?"

He lifted his shoulders. "That was what popped into my head."

Rachel nodded, her hands in the back pockets of her denim. "It's been a while, hasn't it?" Before he could respond, she turned to look around, taking in the clear sky, the lush, serene landscape, the lowing of the cows and the sheep out on the pasture. "So this is *the* Willow Valley you were always talking about. It's very... tranquil, if you don't mind the lack of electricity, or spa saloons." She laughed but underneath the humor, there was derision. "But I do appreciate the lack of traffic. The traffic in Florida has me beat."

He knew he should offer her a cool place to sit but for the life of him, the words would not come out. Had he ever loved this self-centered lady? It was mind-boggling. "What are you doing here, Rachel?"

"Why? Not even a '*I miss you?*' I didn't hurt you that bad."

"I've moved on."

Rachel nodded. "Your letter said as much. That is why I am here."

His letter? *Ach jah.* "We both know there is more to your being here than my letter."

Rachel smiled, latching onto the strap of her leather tote bag. "Maybe I was overcome with the urge to know how you were faring and if truly you were all right."

In other words, *if he was still under her spell.* "As you can see, I am doing very fine."

"And you are happy?" It was a quiet question.

"I am. Very much. Coming home was the best decision I ever made. I met a beautiful, kind-hearted woman and she gives me all the joy in the world."

She made a strangling sound of distress in her throat that he ignored. Reaching out, she placed a hand on the sleeve of his work shirt. "Contrary to what you think, I really do care about you. You must understand – what I did, I did to get your attention. It never felt like you were ever fully with me, if you get my meaning?"

"No. I do not get your meaning." He might have let her get away with manipulating things to favor her in the past, but he was not going to let her get away with it this time. "If you meant to imply that I made you cheat on me with Roy, then maybe you should think about the wisdom of making the trip down here. I will not let you dodge responsibility for your actions. Not this time, Rachel. You cheated because you wanted to, because that is your nature. It wasn't contingent on my attention or lack of it."

"If you had given me the time of day instead of pining after this town and your misplaced sense of loyalty..."

He raised a hand to stop her tirade. "Enough. I didn't leave Florida to subject myself to your endless gaslighting in my own town. There is nothing more to be said. I sent you that letter to grant the both of us closure, not for you to take it as a ground for rekindling anything. I am sorry if I gave you any impression beyond a closed chapter to a story but that is it. Nothing more. And believe me, I appreciate you coming all the way out here to see me. But, really, there is nothing that needs to be said that hasn't already been."

She nodded, reluctantly admitting the bitter truth; that he had finally found his place in the world, and it wasn't with her.

Levi gave her a ride back to town where she was staying the night in the guest house. Tomorrow, she would catch a cab to the airport and return to Florida, where she belonged.

Now, he knew. Sending that letter was cathartic. And the closure well worth it.

Chapter 10

"She'll be so pleased to hear this!"

The high pitch of her mother's animated voice reverberated in the four walls of the living room. Carefully, Katie let the back door slide close without causing too much of a stir. If she was right, then Levi was in the house with her.

The thought sent bittersweet sentiments into the recesses of her mind. She had been trying to put some distance between her and the man. How was she to avoid him if he was in her home?

It didn't help that her mother sounded so happy about his presence. Levi had been paying frequent visits to her over the last few weeks and somehow, he was able to get *Mamm* to warm up to him.

But that was before he was sneaking around and setting up clandestine meetings with past lovers! Leah was very explicit in her description of how cozy the two of them got. Katie knew she was being irrational, and that she should just confront him, but she kept waiting for him to bring up the visit. It didn't take her long to realize he had no intention of telling her about any of it. Why did he wish to keep it a secret if he wasn't doing anything wrong?

"Katie!" The voice of her mother cut her out of her thoughts abruptly. She startled and promptly dropped the basket containing the clean laundry. The clothes lay in a heap on the floor.

"Allow me." Two words from the man responsible for her misery. He dropped to his knees and began moving the laundry from the floor to the basket. At her mother's meaningful look, Katie went on her knees. "It's *oll retch*. You may go back to your discussion; I'll finish up here."

"Katie..." his large hand covered hers, but she didn't wait for him. She jerked the basket and fled the room, leaving a few items of clothing still clutched in his hands.

Beth frowned, her large eyes revealing her consternation at her daughter's uncourteous treatment. "Please pardon her manners. I think she has an engagement in town that she forgot about." As if to underline the authenticity of her words, a horse neighed in the backyard. "There she goes. You can leave the laundry; I'll pick it up."

"*Denki.*"

By the time Levi hurried out of the house, Katie was already rushing down the dirt path and turning around the bend. He followed her discreetly. In the town square, people were out on the streets, contests were going strong, and couples were socializing while children continued to run their parents ragged with concern.

Levi finally stopped directly in front of Katie who was attempting to disembark and ignore him at the same time. He extended a hand and she had to clutch it.

"I was wondering how long that was going to take."

"*Denki* for your aid. I best be on my way now. Beth is expecting me at the riding contest."

"You are participating?"

"*Jah*. I am quite *gut* at spurring the draft horses and drivers to victory."

"Wow. I am impressed. But before you go," he pulled her aside under a lone tarp and out of the street. "Why are you acting so grumpy with me? You've been avoiding me for days; you won't talk to me. You won't even look me in the eye."

"Why were you visiting with my *mamm*?"

Levi frowned. Was that what had her upset? The fact that he didn't check in with her before calling on her mother. "I wanted to discuss something in private with her."

"But why?" she insisted.

"I don't understand. Why – in what way?"

"Why are you bothering? *Mamm* told me you asked for her blessing to court me."

Levi nodded. "*Jah*. I did and she gave her blessing."

"But why?" she cried. "If you are only going to break my heart, why go to all the trouble?"

She wasn't making much sense to him. He told her so and she decided to be direct about her query. "About a week ago, you received a visitor. A strange female visitor. And by the looks of things, it appeared the two of you were more than friends." She watched his expression carefully for any slip-up. "What astounds me is that you think you can keep it a secret in Willow Valley. I heard the gossip even before your lady love left town."

Ah. They were finally at the crux of the matter. "First of all, Rachel is not my lady love. Secondly, I didn't tell you about the visit because it was inconsequential. It wasn't worth discussing. I wrote a letter to the lady informing her about *you*. She made the trip here under her own assumptions; assumptions that I, in no way, bolstered. I set her straight and that was it. She's gone, out of my life just the way I want it. To think that you've been holding a grudge because of that is laughable."

Katie felt silly. The afternoon sun shone brightly, illuminating the beads of sweat on the faces of the passersby, and participants. Under the tarp, it felt like they were enshrouded by a wrap, cut off from the rest of the world. "*Ich...ich...*" The words weren't coming together because she didn't know what to say. She had been so sure something was going on and that he was keeping a secret from her. "You should have still told me. You should have given me the option of deciding whether the meeting was in fact inconsequential." Katie's anger had drained away, but she was still clinging to the fumes of the emotion.

"I didn't feel the need to bring it up. It was of little importance to me so why should I broach the subject with you? I just wish you had approached me with your concerns. I could have saved you a whole lot of stress."

"What did she want?"

"She wanted me back, but I wasn't having any of it. I told her I finally found someone to call mine. Someone I could settle down with, be happy with. That is *you*, Katie, in case you are under any illusions just what you mean to me. *Ich lieba dich.*"

Tears rushed into her eyes. "I love you, too. I am so sorry for ever doubting you. I was being foolish."

"I know, right?" He laughed and pulled her into his arms. "You never have to doubt my love for you, you know?"

"*Jah.*" She smiled tremulously through the tears. "I know it."

Epilogue

♥

Winter rolled into Willow Valley like an avenging angel, enveloping the landscape and hills in a show of white-capped carpet spread everywhere you looked. The snow fell thick and heavy, creating a blanket of white over the fields and farms. The air was crisp and cold, and the sky was a canvas of deep blue. The wind was strong, blowing the snow into drifts and creating a bit of a chill in the air.

Willow Valley residents were slowing down and focusing on indoor activities as the cold weather made it difficult to do farm work, so they focused on indoor tasks such as woodworking, quilting, and other handiwork to keep busy.

Mamm Beth was paying a visit to the *nochbers*, making jam and jellies to share amongst themselves. Katie's brother would be returning home for a long spell after winter, and she was ecstatic. She had written him once or twice in the last few months and mentioned her *beau* and how they would be getting married the following fall season.

Levi lifted her into the sleigh and together, they drove through the deserted streets, hands clutched under the thick lab robes on their thighs.

The smell of woodsmoke in the air, the sound of horses pulling sleighs through the snow and the taste of hot cocoa on a cold day made the experience complete.

"Where are we going?" she asked. She soon had her answer when Levi pulled the horses to a stop in front of her bakery. Her assistant, Theo was there, holding the key in his hands. He opened the door and bade them farewell, leaving the two lovebirds to themselves.

Katie came to a halt when Levi stepped aside. In front of her was the most beautiful artwork. It was made in the finest oakwood and the embellishments along the body were fascinating. It was a display glass and she remembered Levi joking about it some time ago. He explained he wanted everybody to see how good of a baker she was at first glance and this excellent piece of craftmanship would show off her culinary creation to perfection.

"This is *wunderbar! Denki, denki.*" She practically jumped on her feet, gave him a kiss on his cheek, and pirouetted around the display glass. "I *chust* love it."

"I am glad to see you love it. All the blisters in the world are worth seeing that smile on your face." He laughed and twirled her around in his arms. "*Kumm*, I want to show you something."

They got into the sleigh and Levi drove them to Willow Creek. The water was partially frozen, with large chunks of ice floating on the surface. Snowflakes blanketed the banks of the creek, and the surrounding trees were covered in a layer of frost. In the distance, the hills were magically dusted with snow, creating a peaceful and picturesque scene. The quiet stillness of the winter air made the atmosphere heavy with breathless anticipation of what was to come.

"It's so beautiful," Katie said quietly, not wanting to distort the tranquility in the atmosphere. She rubbed her hand-gloved hands absent-mindedly.

"It is funny that I never found anything else to be this serene during my Rumspringa."

"Love brought you back." Katie made the statement boldly.

"And love is going to keep me here." Out of nowhere, he dropped to one knee. "Will you make me the happiest *mann* on Earth and marry me?" He produced a simple, yet elegant handcrafted ring – another one of his handcrafts, *It was stunning.*

"*Jah. Jah,* I will marry you." In her excitement, she jumped into his arms and together they rolled in the snow, laughing and giggling.

The landscape of white-capped mountains and a dewy creek made a backdrop of a fairytale romance story and the ambiance of love completed it.

They had a fall wedding. The wedding was a truly spectacular sight. The leaves were changing colors from green to shades of red, orange, and yellow, creating a stunning backdrop for the wedding that was situated by the creek side where Levi proposed to Katie. The air was crisp and cool, and one could hear leaves rustling in the wind. The setting sun cast a golden glow over the whole scene, creating a sense of warmth and magic.

More than the stunning outdoors, the magical words that the couple exchanged would forever live on in the hearts of the guests.

"Ich schwöre, dich zu lieben und zu ehren, bis das Ende meiner Tage..." I promise to love and honor you, until the end of my days.

Bischop John presided over the wedding and told the couple to recite the words of their solemn marital declarations.

"Ich liebe dich mein lieb, für immer und ewig." I love you, my love, forever and always.

These were the sweet vows that were exchanged with such heartfelt emotion that they brought tears to the eyes of many of the guests.

As the day wore on, lanterns were lit to create a cozy and welcoming ambiance. Dishes were served buffet-style, and there were large cauldrons of soup and stews on the table. Desserts included pies, cakes, cookies, and wedding nothings.

Katie looked around, happy to be surrounded by family and loved ones who had eventually opened up to Levi and accepted him as one of their own. Even Jacob was here, and he seemed to be having fun, with one of the *Englishers* who had come home with Joshua, Katie's brother.

Vell, that was a story for another time.

Right now, Katie was too happy to look anywhere but at her own *mann.*

And so began the rest of their happily ever after, with love, faith, and hope for the bright future to come.

About Sadie Weaver

Thank you so much for reading my book! I hope you loved the story.

Sign up for my newsletter and get *Abigail's Amish Heart*, an exclusive just for my readers.

I love to hear from you, so don't be shy! If you'd like to connect directly please feel free to visit my Facebook page:

https://www.facebook.com/sadieweaverauthor

Or email me at: **sadie@sadieweaver.com**

Made in the USA
Coppell, TX
31 July 2024

35418399R00069